Welcome to the Fairy House –
a whole new magical world…

Have you got all *The Fairy House* books?

- ☐ FAIRY FRIENDS
- ☐ FAIRY FOR A DAY
- ☐ FAIRIES TO THE RESCUE
- ☐ FAIRY RIDING SCHOOL
- ☐ FAIRY SLEEPOVER
- ☐ FAIRY JEWELS
- ☐ FAIRY PARTY
- ☐ FAIRY FLYING LESSONS

Make sure you visit www.thefairyhouse.co.uk
for competitions, prizes and lots more fairy fun!

Kelly McKain

Illustrated by Nicola Slater

SCHOLASTIC

First published in the UK in 2007 by Scholastic Children's Books
An imprint of Scholastic Ltd
Euston House, 24 Eversholt Street
London, NW1 1DB, UK
Registered office: Westfield Road, Southam, Warwickshire, CV47 0RA

This edition published in 2009

ISBN 978 1 407 10887 2

A CIP catalogue record for this book is available from the British Library

Printed in the UK by CPI Bookmarque, Croydon, CR0 4TD
Papers used by Scholastic Children's Books are made
from wood grown in sustainable forests.

1 3 5 7 9 10 8 6 4 2

www.kellymckain.co.uk
www.scholastic.co.uk/zone

For

Chloe and Gabrielle, with love

With thanks to

Amanda Punter, Katy Moran, Elaine McQuade, Andrew Biscomb, Georgia Lawe, Sarah Spedding, Kate Wilson, Claire Tagg, Eleanor Schramm, and Hilary Murray-Hill for working your magic on this, and for loving Fairy House as much as I do! xx

Chapter 1

Katie skipped ahead of Mum all the way home from school, trying to get her to walk faster. As they rounded the corner into the newly built close, she felt her heart leap with excitement. The houses were all the same, small and brown, like tiny Lego boxes – well, almost. Katie was proud that theirs stood out from the crowd. Mum, an artist, loved all things bright and beautiful, so she'd painted the front door a vivid pink.

But it wasn't the house that Katie was excited about. She just couldn't wait to meet up with her four new friends. Once inside, she hurried through the living room and kitchen, dropping her school bag on the way. She was heading for the back door, but Mum made her sit down and have some orange juice and a home-made flapjack first. Then she was gone, dashing across the garden and under the wire that separated their boring square patch of lawn from the overgrown, wild-flower-strewn almost-meadow that lay beyond. Katie swished through the tall grass, thick with dandelions and poppies, humming a

song that one of her new friends had taught her.

As she reached the oak tree and saw the dolls' house beneath it, she couldn't help smiling.

Although it was just like any other, it certainly wasn't ordinary. Incredible as it sounded, Katie's new friends lived *inside* it – and they were *fairies*.

When Katie had first seen them, she'd hardly believed her eyes.

She'd left the dolls' house outside one night under the old oak tree, and when she returned the next morning she got a big surprise! Four tiny fairies called Bluebell, Daisy, Rosehip and Snowdrop had moved in!

Together, Katie and the fairies had transformed the pink plastic dolls' house into a beautiful home. Bluebell had decorated the walls with pressed-flower pictures and there were rose-petal covers on the sofas and polka-dot curtains at the windows. They'd even made a string of tiny sparkling fairy lights to keep the house cheerful at night.

Then Katie had painted the words "The Fairy House" on the front door in lovely swirly letters and given it to the fairies for their very own. Luckily Mum had allowed her to keep it under the oak tree in the almost-meadow.

Katie loved the way the Fairy House was becoming part of the landscape, with Snowdrop's wonderful window boxes cascading

with pink and purple flowers, and the grass growing taller around it as summer settled in.

Daisy and Snowdrop popped their heads out of Bluebell's bedroom window and waved to Katie. "Hurray! You're back!" Daisy cried.

"Come on in!" added Snowdrop. "You'll have to shrink first, of course!"

Katie grinned at them – she was really looking forward to more fairy fun! She crouched down beside the Fairy House and pressed the tip of her little finger on to the tiny blue door handle, which Bluebell had bewitched with fairy dust.

"I believe in fairies, I believe in fairies, I believe in fairies," she whispered. She gasped in delight as the top of her head tingled. Then a

great whooshing sound roared in her ears and everything around her seemed to be getting bigger and bigger and bigger. But, of course, she was getting smaller and smaller and smaller. And suddenly she was fairy sized! Just as she was about to go inside, Bluebell and Rosehip came whizzing round the tree. Bluebell was flying determinedly ahead, with Rosehip close behind, reaching out to grab her foot.

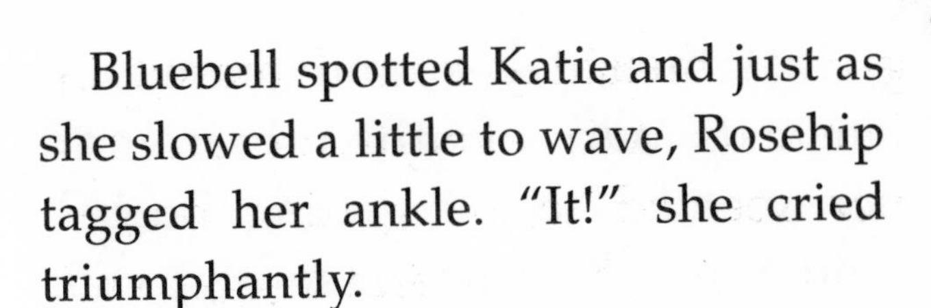

Bluebell spotted Katie and just as she slowed a little to wave, Rosehip tagged her ankle. "It!" she cried triumphantly.

"That wasn't fair!" shouted Bluebell, hovering in mid-air with her hands on her hips. "I only slowed down to say hello to Katie!"

Rosehip tossed her fiery orange hair and did a mocking loop-the-loop. "We were still playing so it *does* count, actually," she cried. "You're it! Ha ha!" And with that, she zoomed past Bluebell, sticking out her tongue.

Bluebell lunged at Rosehip and Katie laughed as the two fairies became a shrieking ball of fluttering wings and flailing legs. They were the best of friends, but they also had hot tempers and were always falling out!

Just then, Daisy and Snowdrop rushed out of the door and swamped Katie in hugs. Bluebell and Rosehip came crashing to the ground, leapt up and brushed themselves down, the squabble forgotten. All smiles, they joined in the hug.

"We've made a skipping rope with woven grass," Snowdrop said, pulling a long rope from the pocket of her dress for Katie to see. "Will you play with us?"

"Of course," said Katie, "but first I have to tell you something – something very important. It's about your fairy task."

As soon as Katie said this, Snowdrop reached into the pocket of her dress again and pulled out the scroll they'd been given by the Fairy Queen herself. It said:

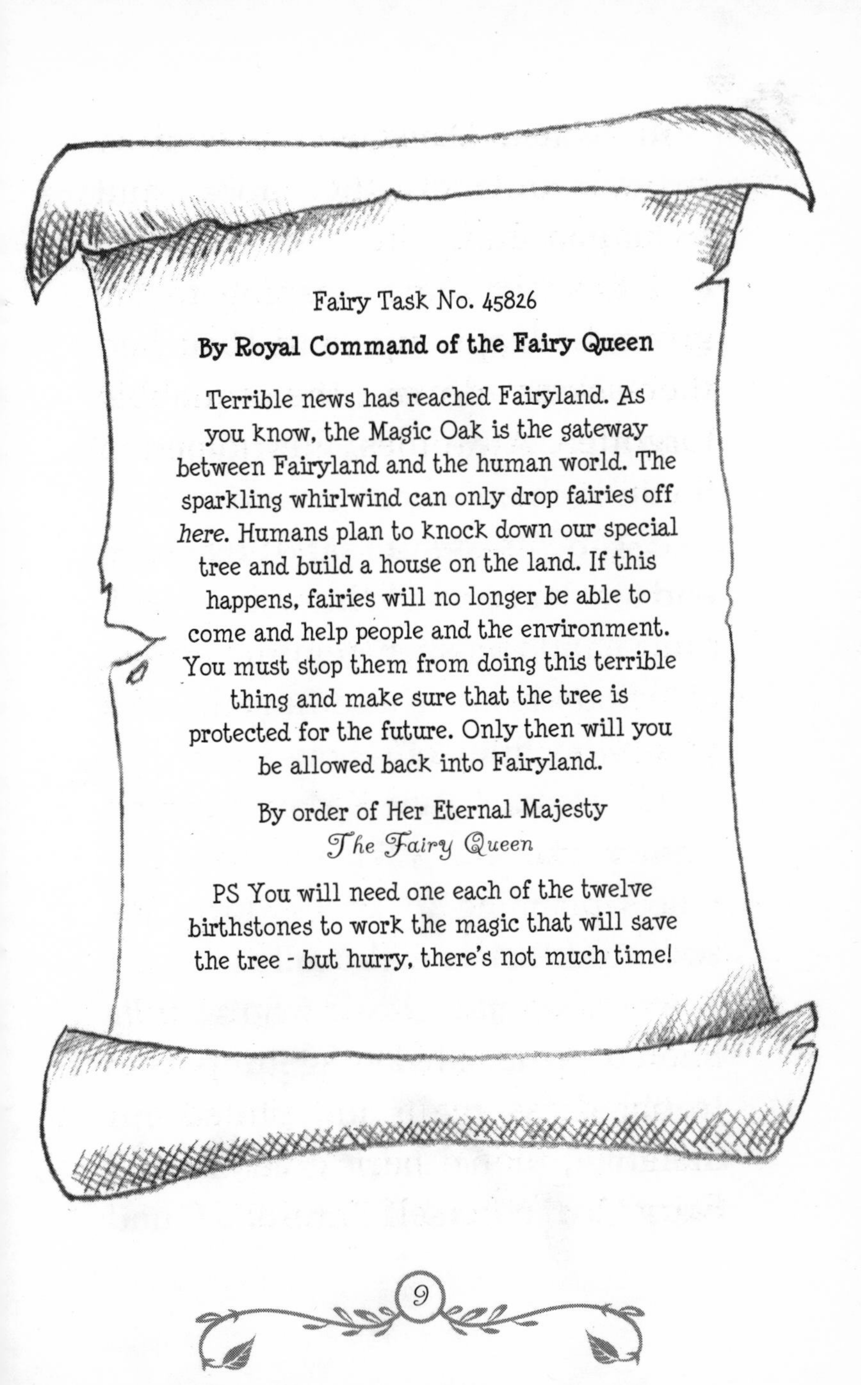

Fairy Task No. 45826

By Royal Command of the Fairy Queen

Terrible news has reached Fairyland. As you know, the Magic Oak is the gateway between Fairyland and the human world. The sparkling whirlwind can only drop fairies off *here*. Humans plan to knock down our special tree and build a house on the land. If this happens, fairies will no longer be able to come and help people and the environment. You must stop them from doing this terrible thing and make sure that the tree is protected for the future. Only then will you be allowed back into Fairyland.

By order of Her Eternal Majesty
The Fairy Queen

PS You will need one each of the twelve birthstones to work the magic that will save the tree - but hurry, there's not much time!

Katie had been given a ring by her Auntie Jane, which turned out to be garnet, the January stone. So they'd found one at least, but they still needed eleven others. Katie had got a book out of the library and read up on the twelve birthstones. Some of them were very expensive, like ruby, sapphire and emerald, and she had no idea how they'd lay their hands on such gems.

"I found out from Mum that the man who built our house and this whole close is called Max Towner," Katie explained. "I'll bet he's the one who's planning to knock down the tree! And there's a girl called Tiffany Towner in my class, who's *really* horrible and always getting into trouble. Mum said she's his daughter." The fairies all looked impressed with what Katie had found

out. "The problem is that Tiffany won't talk to me, because she thinks I'm a goody-goody," Katie continued. "I wanted to ask about her dad's plans, so I sat with her at lunch today, but she just ignored me."

"There is another way we could find out about Tiffany's father's plans," Daisy said slowly, a thoughtful look on her face. "One of *us* could make friends with her."

Katie stared at her, astonished. "But how?"

"By turning big and going to school instead of you!" said Bluebell excitedly.

"We could pretend it was an exchange day so she wouldn't be suspicious," added Snowdrop.

"What a great idea!" cried Katie. "But how do you turn big? Do you just use a sprinkling of fairy dust?"

There was a silence.

"Well?" Katie prompted. She realized that the fairies were all glancing at each other nervously from under their long eyelashes.

"Erm, not exactly *just* a sprinkling of fairy dust," said Daisy reluctantly, fiddling with her long plaits. "There is a price to pay. For a fairy to

become a human, a human has to become a fairy, to take her place."

"You mean *me*?" Katie gasped, eyes gleaming with excitement.

"It takes courage," Daisy warned. "If something happened to one of you, the other would be stuck the wrong size for ever. Or if one of you didn't want to turn back afterwards, the other one couldn't. It's not something to be taken lightly."

All the fairies looked hopefully up at Katie, who stood perfectly still, feeling stunned. It was riskier than she'd thought – what if she got stuck as a fairy? She'd miss school, and Auntie Jane, and worst of all Mum would never see her again! She couldn't even *begin* to imagine how awful that would be!

But then she remembered the fairies' task, and how she'd

promised to help them in any way she could. If the tree were knocked down it would spell disaster for earth as well as Fairyland. Fairies looked after the seasons, and all the plants, trees and flowers. Without them there might be snow in June, or maybe constant rain, or perhaps the fruit and vegetables wouldn't grow and there would be nothing to eat. They could only imagine what the consequences would be – but one thing was certain, they wouldn't be good! Katie took a deep breath and stood up. "We have to find out if Max Towner is behind this plan to knock down the tree," she said, "and this is the best chance we have. I'll do it."

"Oh, Katie, thanks!" cried Daisy.

"Well done!" added Snowdrop.

Bluebell suddenly stood up. "I'll

do it too," she announced, and they all whirled round to stare at her. But no one said thank you or well done this time. In fact, no one said anything!

"What's the matter?" asked Bluebell.

"Don't take this the wrong way," said Daisy finally, in her gentlest voice, "but you'll never be able to keep calm with Tiffany. What if she says nasty things about Katie?"

"I'll control my temper," Bluebell promised. "As Katie says, we have to find out if Tiffany's dad is behind these wicked plans, and quickly. Besides, it'll be fun, like being a secret agent and

going undercover – I'll blend right in."

Katie giggled and clamped her hand over her mouth.

"What? What's so funny about that?" Bluebell demanded.

"You won't blend in with that blue hair!" Katie told her. "But if you're sure you can handle Tiffany, I'm willing to switch with you. You're very brave, Bluebell."

Bluebell did a twirl of pride and finished it off with a curtsey.

"I was going to volunteer too," Rosehip grumbled.

"Bluebell offered first, so it's only fair that she should turn big," Daisy told her. "We'll all need to go to school anyway, to

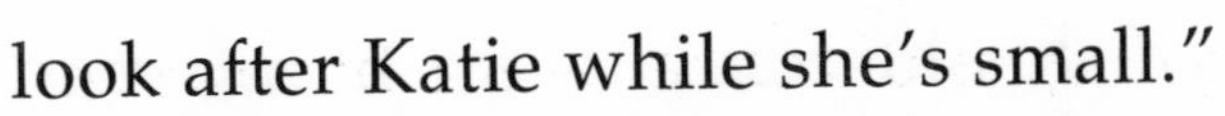

look after Katie while she's small."

"Still not fair," Rosehip huffed, but she didn't say anything more.

"So we're agreed," said Katie. "Tomorrow we swap places!" She lunged over to hug Bluebell and they had an excited jumping-up-and-downy squealy hug and dance around together, which the others soon joined in, even Rosehip. While the risks worried her, Katie was impossibly excited about becoming a fairy, even just for one day!

"I have to go in for tea soon," she said breathlessly, when they finally broke apart. "But there's just time for a turn with your new skipping rope, Snowdrop."

Snowdrop beamed at her and unravelled the rope. Rosehip made up a special fairy skipping song

which she taught them all, and pretty soon, she and Katie were in together, chanting, "Flap your wings and stomp your feet, jump in, Bluebell, don't miss a beat!" as Bluebell jumped in too.

The chant made Katie feel extra excited – after all, tomorrow she would be flapping her own wings,

not just singing about it! She'd be a *real* fairy!

The skipping was so much fun that Katie almost forgot the time, until her rumbling tummy reminded her. Worried that Mum would come out looking for her and she'd be nowhere to be

seen, she gave her fairy friends a quick goodbye hug.

For tea they shared one of Mum's home-made pizzas (Katie knew that Mum hid all kinds of vegetables under the cheese, but somehow it was still delicious!). Then after she'd helped with the drying up, Katie dug out her own skipping rope and asked Mum to play with her. They tied one end to the door handle and took turns at the other, and Katie couldn't resist singing Rosehip's skipping song.

"What a lovely tune," Mum remarked. "Where did you learn that?"

"Oh, my new friends sing it, at erm, school," mumbled Katie.

Mum beamed. "I'm so glad you're settling in so well, darling," she

said, and, grinning, she began to turn the rope faster and faster.

Katie giggled, feet flying. "Mum, stop it!" she cried, not meaning a word.

Katie felt bad for fibbing to Mum, even just a little tiny bit, but she had *tried* to tell her the truth about the fairies when she'd first met them. The problem was that, like most grown-ups, Mum didn't believe in fairies and couldn't see them, so she just thought Katie was talking about imaginary friends she'd invented!

Later that evening, Katie had her bath and did her reading as usual, and soon she was all snuggled up in bed. But she was just too excited to sleep!

Eventually she got up and crept over to her window. Squinting into

the darkness she could just make out the Fairy House, glowing with the daisy lights she'd helped to make. Although she couldn't see into its tiny windows, she had a feeling Bluebell was still awake too, gazing out into the almost-meadow, looking forward to her big day.

Chapter 2

The next morning as Mum walked Katie in to school, she had no idea that four little fairies were coming too! They were flying along at Katie's shoulder, wings shimmering in the sunlight, eyes shining with excitement.

As they neared the school, the fairies took cover in the front pockets of Katie's school bag, with just their heads poking out.

When Bluebell spotted some girls skipping in the playground she cried out, "Wow, maybe I'll get to do skipping when I'm big. Big skipping looks even more fun than fairy skipping!"

"I bet you won't!" said Rosehip, and Katie realized that she was still jealous of Bluebell getting to be big instead of her. She hoped it wouldn't spoil their exciting day.

Once Mum said goodbye, Katie and the fairies hurried to the changing rooms to do the swap. It was always registration in their classrooms first thing, so no one ever went near them before school.

Katie took off her school tie and tossed it on to a peg. Then she put her bag down on the floor and the fairies flew out.

She was really nervous, with butterflies in her stomach and jelly for legs. From the queasy look on Bluebell's face, she wasn't feeling much better!

Katie lay flat on her stomach on the floor in front of Bluebell, and tried to banish her worries from her mind. Snowdrop pulled the bottle of fairy dust from her huge pocket and sprinkled a little on each of their hands. Squeezing their eyes shut,

Katie and Bluebell touched palms. There was an instant zapping feeling, like a spark of lightning rushing between them, and then a loud POP!

Katie leapt up from the floor and found herself the same size as Snowdrop. She did a twirl and fluttered her wings. "It worked!" she cried. "I'm a *real* fairy!"

"And I'm a *real* girl!" Bluebell gasped.

Katie smiled up at her friend – and noticed that she was now the same height as Bluebell's ankle!

Although they had to hurry in to class, Katie couldn't resist

trying a little flight. At first she thought she wouldn't know how to do it, but it turned out to be as simple as reaching out for a glass of milk. She *wanted* to fly so the wings just fluttered slightly and up she went! Even being just a couple of centimetres off the ground was scary, though. She realized that it would take a while before she was doing somersaults and acrobatics in the air like the others!

Then the bell went, making them all jump. Snowdrop clamped her hands over her ears and pulled a face.

"We'd better go," Katie called up to Bluebell, "or you'll be late."

"I'm not being ordered around by bells!" Bluebell shouted back. She stamped her foot, making Katie and the fairies dive out of the way.

"Careful, Bluebell," shrieked Daisy in alarm.

"Oh sorry!" cried Bluebell. "I forgot how big I was! It's just that I hate bells. If someone wants me to do something they can come in here and ask me nicely!"

Katie groaned. "You've got a lot to learn about school, Bluebell!" she said. "You *have* to listen to the bells. Look, just do your best to fit in with the others and keep out of trouble, won't you?"

"Don't worry," said Bluebell. "I'll be brilliant, you'll see. They'll never guess that I'm any different to the other children." With that she took Katie's tie off the peg and proudly put it on. Katie decided not to mention that it was skew-whiff – Bluebell was so excited to be going to school and she didn't want

anything to spoil her friend's big day.

Then the other fairies leapt into the school bag and helped Katie to climb in too.

"All aboard," cried Bluebell, swinging the bag on to her shoulder so enthusiastically they all screamed. Now that she was fairy-sized, it felt like a fairground ride to Katie!

They grew more and more excited as Bluebell strode down the corridor, with Katie giving directions from the pocket of her school bag. Then, "Good luck," she added, as they reached the classroom.

Bluebell smiled thanks at her, then they all bobbed down. If some of the children believed in fairies,

they might be able to see them.

When they were safely out of sight, Bluebell took a deep breath, crossed her fingers for luck and opened the classroom door.

Chapter 3

Mrs Borthwick, Katie's teacher, was a cheerful woman with a blunt-cut grey bob and bobbly leggings under a big orange shirt. She'd been teaching so long that the oddest of odd things didn't usually surprise her, but even *she* was a little startled to see a complete stranger with a silky petal skirt, wonky school tie and bright blue hair come marching through her classroom door.

"Hello, dear," she said kindly. "What can I do for you?"

When Bluebell explained that she and Katie had done a day's exchange, Mrs Borthwick looked doubtful. But the little bit of fairy dust Snowdrop threw into the air around them soon made her believe it!

Blinking the fairy dust from her eyes, Mrs Borthwick welcomed Bluebell to the class and asked her to take Katie's seat. She told her that Katie's partner Chloe was off with a tummy bug, so Bluebell scooted over to sit by the window, which was wide open to the June breeze. She propped a maths book

up against the sill and the fairies climbed gratefully out of the bag and hid behind it. They hated being cooped up, as Katie had found out when she'd tried to bring them into her house!

Bluebell didn't have to ask Katie who Tiffany was, because a whining voice called out, "Why doesn't *she* have to put her bag in the cloakroom like everyone else, Miss?"

Bluebell whirled round in her seat to see a girl with scraggly brown hair and a pink face giving her a mean stare.

"Now, Tiffany, Bluebell is our guest and she's only here for one day," said Mrs Borthwick. "They probably have different rules at her school." She turned to Bluebell and smiled kindly. "Don't they, dear?"

Bluebell nodded. "Yes, Miss, we keep all our things in our desks at school, because it's very difficult to fly with a bag of heavy books. If one of your wings gets trapped, you can fall right out of the air!"

Mrs Borthwick beamed at her. "How lovely that you like inventing stories, just like Katie!" she exclaimed.

"Oh, it's not a story, Miss," Bluebell insisted. "It's true."

Mrs Borthwick raised her eyebrows then. "Anyway, sit down dear and we'll all get on with the lesson," she said, a little sharply.

But Tiffany didn't want to get on with the lesson. Tiffany wanted to pick on Bluebell a bit more. "It's not fair that *she's* got blue hair, Miss!" she whinged. "No one's allowed to dye their hair at *this* school!"

Furious, Bluebell leapt up from her seat and went crashing across the classroom to Tiffany's desk. "It's not dyed, it's real!" she shouted.

"Liar, liar! Pants on fire!" chanted Tiffany, with a nasty sneer on her face.

"Bluebell, sit down at once,"

ordered Mrs Borthwick, her usual cheery tone gone.

Bluebell stamped back to her place but she couldn't resist twisting round in her seat to stick her tongue out at Tiffany. Katie poked her head over the maths book, wearing the graph paper disguise Snowdrop had just made her. It completely covered her face, except for two tiny eyeholes. "Bluebell, stop that!" she hissed. "You're supposed to be making friends with her!"

"Oops! Sorry!" whispered Bluebell. "I will try. It's just that she's so horrible!"

"I said she would be, and you promised to hold your temper," Katie reminded her, before ducking down again.

When the class went to assembly,

Katie had a chance to practise her flying in the empty classroom. Under Daisy's guidance she tried a few leaps into the air and a bit of hovering. When she'd got the hang of that, she had a go at flying from desk to desk. Rosehip held her hand at first, then after a few turns she felt brave enough to try it all on her own. Soon she was zooming round the classroom, looping the loop and doing cartwheels in the air with the others. "Wow! This is the best feeling ever!" she cried, her heart soaring.

Then they heard the piano strike up for the end-of-assembly song – and a booming voice bellowing out the wrong words, accompanied by the wrong tune – and very VERY LOUDLY! They all looked at each other in horror. "Bluebell!" they gasped.

Katie groaned. "She'll really need to start fitting in soon," she said. "Or she'll never be able to make friends with Tiffany!"

Soon the class returned and Katie and the fairies took cover on the window sill. A few moments later, the children were sitting cross-legged on the carpet at the front of the room, ready for their first lesson. Four little heads peeked around the side of the maths book, all their fingers crossed, necks craning to spot Bluebell. But suddenly their friend's head appeared above them, leaning far out of the window, taking deep breaths!

"Bluebell!" Katie hissed, as they all ducked down. "You can't just—"

But Tiffany's voice came whimpering across the classroom. "Miss, look what she's doing!" she wailed.

Everyone turned to stare and the room exploded with laughter.

"Bluebell, come and sit down at once!" bellowed Mrs Borthwick.

"I only wanted some fresh air," Bluebell mumbled, red-faced with embarrassment. Then she hurried to sit down on the carpet with everyone else.

Katie watched Mrs Borthwick take what Mum called a "deep cleansing breath".

"Now, children, today we're going to talk about healthy eating," she began. "So, who has a favourite food?"

A few of the children put their hands up, but before Mrs Borthwick could choose someone, Bluebell shouted out cheerfully, "*I* don't, Miss! I don't eat food! I live on love and laughter!"

Everyone burst out laughing again and poor Bluebell looked startled.

Mrs Borthwick frowned at her. "Could you put your hand up if you want to answer, please, dear?" she said wearily. "And don't make up silly things."

"But I'm not! It's true!" Bluebell insisted. Then she went into a huge sulk at the unfairness of it all, and said nothing for the rest of the lesson. She even seemed to forget her task, and didn't smile at Tiffany once!

Peeking over the maths book, Katie grimaced – this was not going as well as she'd hoped. In fact it was not going well *at all*.

"*I* could have done far better than her," Rosehip whispered, with satisfaction.

"I'm just glad it's not me in there," said Snowdrop, shuddering.

"Maybe I should have persuaded her not to do it," added Daisy, frowning.

"No, it's *my* fault," Katie insisted. "I should have told her more about humans, and how to behave at school."

At break time, and after several more tellings-off, Bluebell dragged herself across the playground and sat alone on a secluded bench. Checking that the coast was clear, Katie and the other fairies flew over to join her. As Daisy, Snowdrop and Rosehip played flying "It" round the bench, Katie tried to give Bluebell some emergency training on how to behave at school. "Just try to remember about putting your hand up and not shouting out," she advised, "and do your best to think of human answers to questions instead of fairy

ones, and most importantly of all – don't stick your head out of the window!"

Katie thought Bluebell would laugh at this last thing, but she just looked even more upset. "I'm trying really hard," she wailed. "I just don't seem to be getting anything right. Tiffany already thinks I'm awful, she won't tell me anything at this rate! Oh, maybe this isn't going to work after all!" And with that she settled into such a glum mood that it took two of Daisy's best jokes and one of Rosehip's liveliest fairy songs to cheer her up enough to keep on trying.

Luckily, after break it was music and movement, which is the same in Fairyland as it is in the human world. Well, nearly the same... When Mrs Borthwick asked if

Bluebell had a PE kit to change into, she just blinked at her and said that she'd never heard of such a thing, and she'd be staying in her blue skirt, which she'd never ever taken off, not even once!

Mrs Borthwick sighed and told her that it really wasn't nice to lie, and of course Bluebell insisted once again that she was telling the truth.

Peering down through a high window, Katie groaned – the emergency training hadn't sunk in at all!

But Mrs Borthwick didn't stay annoyed with Bluebell for long. Soon the children were in the hall doing promenades and gigs and reels and swing your partner round and round, and she was full of praise for Bluebell's sense of rhythm and light-footedness. The fairies

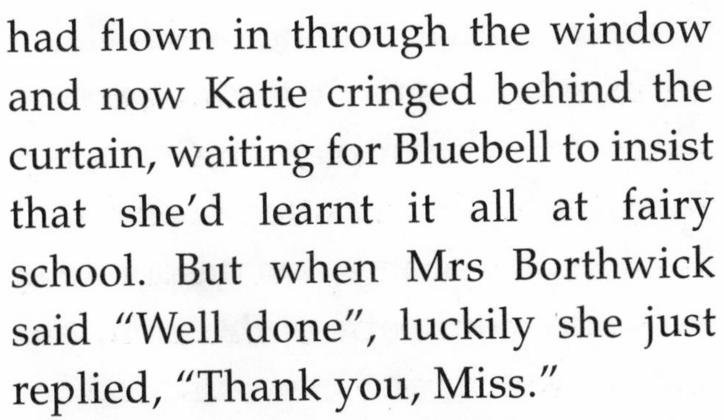

had flown in through the window and now Katie cringed behind the curtain, waiting for Bluebell to insist that she'd learnt it all at fairy school. But when Mrs Borthwick said "Well done", luckily she just replied, "Thank you, Miss."

Katie breathed a sigh of relief – maybe Bluebell was getting the

hang of school after all!

As the class continued, Katie and the fairies peeked longingly round the curtain, tapping their feet.

"I wish *we* could join in," said Snowdrop wistfully.

"Me too," grumbled Rosehip, "I love dancing! Look! Bluebell missed a beat there. I'd be much better at this!"

"Rosehip, try not to be so jealous," said Daisy gently. "We have to support our friend."

Katie knew that Daisy was desperate to zoom into the centre of the room and join in herself, and thought her very kind for still thinking of Bluebell first. Then she suddenly remembered the

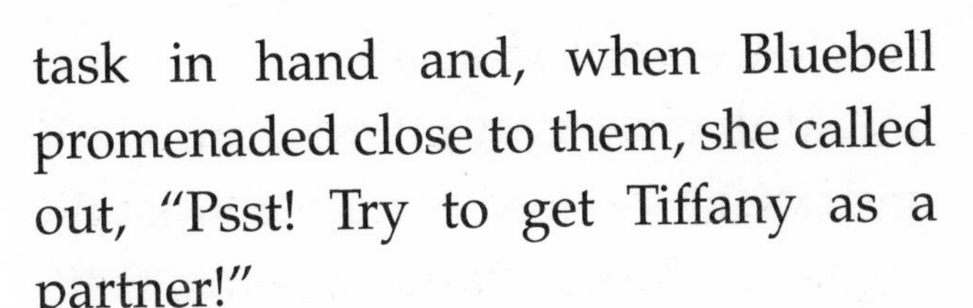

task in hand and, when Bluebell promenaded close to them, she called out, "Psst! Try to get Tiffany as a partner!"

Bluebell heard her and gave her a quick wink and a smile. Then she instantly dropped the hands of her partner, marched across the room and barged Tiffany's partner out of the way!

"Oh no! I didn't mean like that!" Katie cried in despair. "And she was doing so well!"

Mrs Borthwick wasn't happy either and made Bluebell sit out, in trouble again. The next time Tiffany promenaded past Bluebell she gave her a nasty look, and hissed, "Stay away from me! You're a weird girl and your hair is stupid, so there!" She had such spite in her eyes that even brave Bluebell looked shaken and upset.

When everyone was busy practising a new step with Mrs Borthwick, Katie and the fairies fluttered down from the window sill and landed in Bluebell's lap.

Rosehip was about to gloat but the tear rolling down Bluebell's cheek stopped her.

"Oh, I really wanted to do well!" she sniffled, plopping big fat tears on to her friends' heads. "But I'm just messing everything up. I keep getting into trouble and Tiffany hates me. School is definitely not as much fun as I'd imagined!"

They all hugged her waist and, had anyone looked her way at that moment, they'd have thought she was wearing a fluttering, shimmering belt!

"Don't worry," said Katie kindly. "It'll work out, somehow."

At the end of the lesson, Katie and the fairies hurried back to the window sill. All the children lined up, then Mrs Borthwick led them back to the changing rooms to get ready for lunch. Bluebell dragged herself up from the bench miserably, and sloped off to join the end of the line.

Chapter 4

After lunch, Bluebell wandered over to the far end of the field and found a lovely beech tree to sit under. Her friends soon spotted her and flew over. Bluebell looked a lot more cheerful, so they all crowded round, hoping she'd managed to make friends with Tiffany in the dining hall.

"So, what did you find out?" asked Daisy eagerly.

"Well, I found out that human

food is absolutely yummy!" Bluebell giggled. "Oh, you just wouldn't believe it. The taste! There was vegetable pie with cheesy mashed potato that just melted in my mouth, and—"

"Well, if you think school dinners are nice, wait until you try chocolate ice cream, Mum's home-made pizza or fat green grapes!" Katie said, grinning.

Rosehip shook her long flame-bright hair crossly. "Fairies shouldn't eat human food," she announced. "You'll probably get sick soon." Katie noticed that she looked quite cheerful at the thought. Bluebell stuck her tongue

out at her. One of their famous arguments seemed to be brewing, so Katie said quickly, "Any luck with Tiffany?"

Bluebell shook her head sadly. "She sat on another table with her horrid friends and whispered and pointed at me all through lunch. It spoilt my bananas and custard," she muttered, tears in her eyes.

They all looked disappointed and Snowdrop began to cry.

Katie put her arm round her. "Shush, it's OK," she said gently.

"But what if it's not?" sobbed Snowdrop. "What if the bulldozers come tomorrow? We're not ready to work the

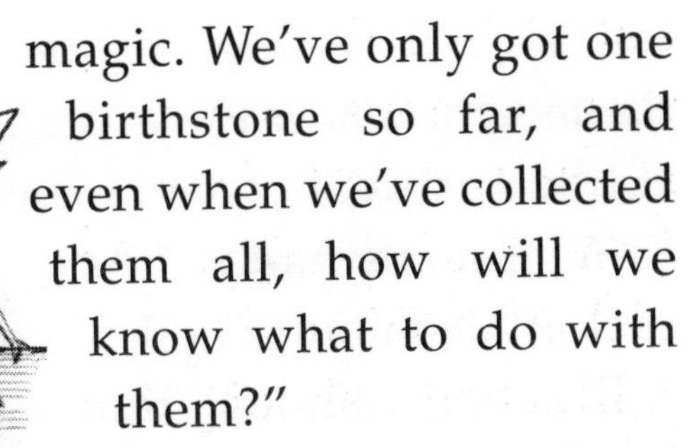

magic. We've only got one birthstone so far, and even when we've collected them all, how will we know what to do with them?"

A thick gloom descended on the little group of friends. Snowdrop had said the very things out loud that they were all secretly frightened about.

"Even if we can't find out who's behind this, we need to keep collecting the birthstones, as the Fairy Queen told us," said Rosehip finally, breaking the silence. "We must be on red alert at all times for chances to find them."

Her friends all nodded in agreement.

"Good thinking, Rosehip," said Katie, who knew it was important to think positively, even when things looked really bad.

Just then the bell went. Katie looked at Bluebell but she didn't move. "Bluebell, you have to go and line up," she prompted.

"No way!" cried Bluebell, stamping her foot. "Tiffany hates me – she'll never tell me anything now! I don't want to spend even one second more with her, and I can't stand any more tellings-off!"

"But it's arts and crafts next," Katie told her. "And we're using beads. I'm just wondering if, maybe—"

"We might find another birth-stone there!" Rosehip interrupted gleefully.

"Yes!" cried Daisy. "The Fairy

Queen works in mysterious ways. *We* think we've only come to school to find out information from Tiffany but maybe Her Eternal Majesty has led us here to find another birthstone as well!"

They all felt a lot more cheerful after that.

Bluebell leapt up. "Right! I'll see if I can spot any birthstones in arts and crafts. Then we can check the changing rooms at home time, and the classroom after school, too. You never know, maybe we'll find one!"

"Good luck!" they chorused, and with that she marched determinedly off across the field.

"And try to remember what I taught you about school!" Katie called after her.

Bluebell turned and grinned at them. "Don't worry, it's all in here,"

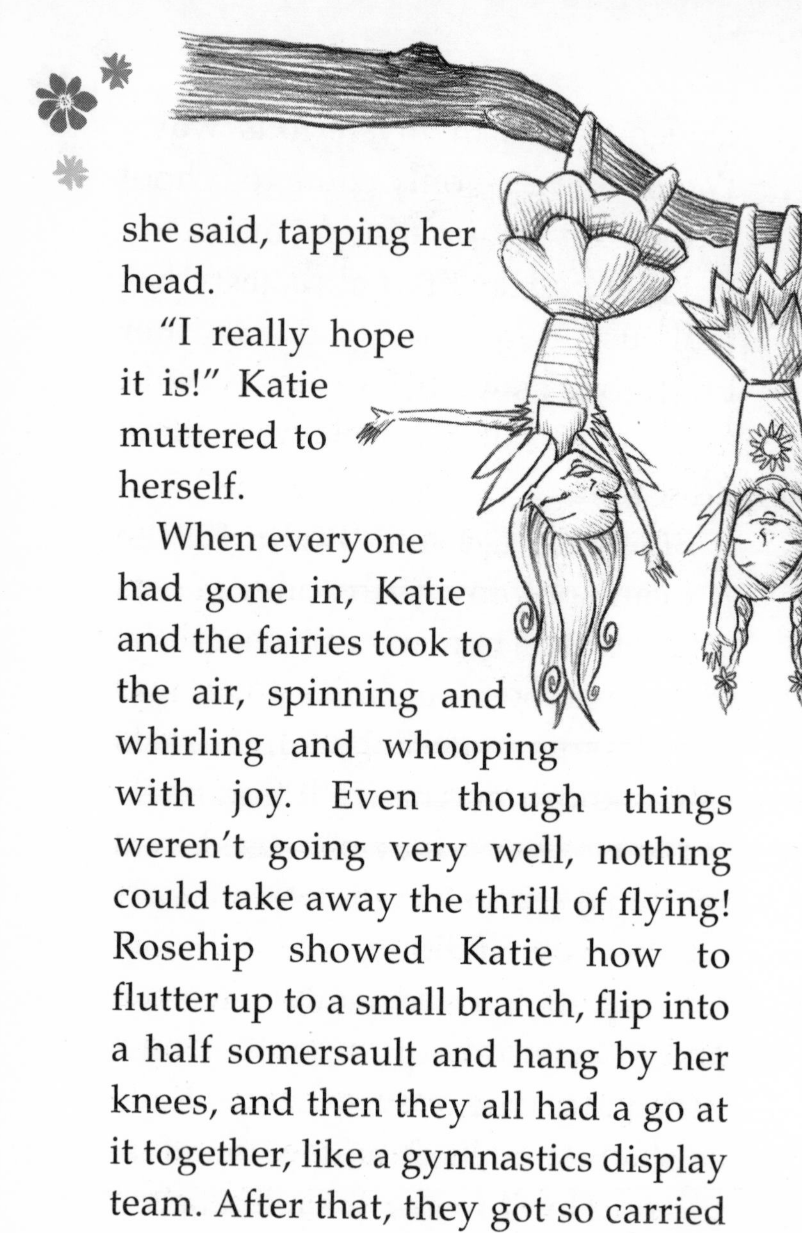

she said, tapping her head.

"I really hope it is!" Katie muttered to herself.

When everyone had gone in, Katie and the fairies took to the air, spinning and whirling and whooping with joy. Even though things weren't going very well, nothing could take away the thrill of flying! Rosehip showed Katie how to flutter up to a small branch, flip into a half somersault and hang by her knees, and then they all had a go at it together, like a gymnastics display team. After that, they got so carried

away with playing "It" in the air that they almost forgot to go and see how Bluebell was getting on in the arts and crafts lesson.

Katie led them back across the field to the school, turning somersaults all the way, and soon the art room was straight ahead. Daisy, Rosehip and Snowdrop touched down with grace and ease, whereas Katie crashed straight into the window-pane and fell to the floor. The other

fairies swooped down to help her up. "Erm, that's something we should have mentioned." Snowdrop said, giggling. "Landings take a bit of practice!"

Grinning, Katie dusted herself off and they fluttered carefully back up into the air and clambered through the open window. The children were all quietly working on their projects, heads down, and a low drone of chatter filled the room. The four friends just needed to find a hiding place – and quickly, before anyone spotted them!

Chapter 5

Katie and the fairies dived down to the art-room floor, then inched along the skirting board and fluttered up to the sink. There they took cover under a pile of paint-smeared palettes that sat waiting to be washed. They blended in so well with all the brightly-coloured paint, it was like camouflage. Then they spotted Bluebell, sitting next to one of the nice girls in Katie's class (definitely not Tiffany!). She

was cheerfully threading beads on to a string.

Katie watched as the children picked beads out from pots in the centre of each table. Some were making necklaces, others worked on beaded sword-hilts or clay goblets and a few stuck the beads on to card to make mosaics. "This is just the right place to find another

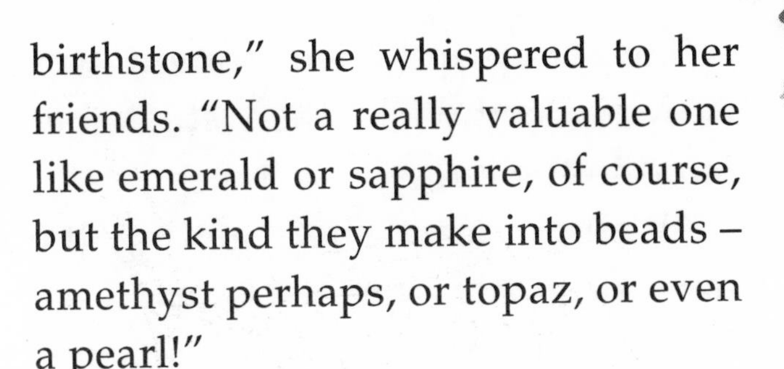

birthstone," she whispered to her friends. "Not a really valuable one like emerald or sapphire, of course, but the kind they make into beads – amethyst perhaps, or topaz, or even a pearl!"

Bluebell was frantically hunting in the pots and Katie knew that she was trying to find a birthstone. She just hoped that she'd remember how to behave – if she was accidentally naughty and got banned from arts and crafts it would spell disaster!

"Oh, those necklaces look so beautiful!" whispered Rosehip. "It's so unfair! *I* want to make one!"

"Me too," said Snowdrop ruefully.

They waved and waved from the sink until Bluebell finally noticed them.

She got up and went straight over to Mrs Borthwick, then stuck her hand in the air.

"Well, at least she's getting the hang of putting her hand up," said Katie, "sort of!"

"Yes, dear?" said Mrs Borthwick, smiling kindly.

"May I wash my hands, Miss?" Bluebell asked politely.

"Certainly, dear," said Mrs Borthwick, looking pleased with her at last.

When she came over to the sink, Daisy whispered, "Any luck?"

"Before you came in, I asked Mrs Borthwick where all the beads came from. She said that they're mostly plastic, but that there are a few from some old broken necklaces," Bluebell said excitedly. "She couldn't quite remember, but she

thought one of them might have been topaz, which is. . ."

"One of the birthstones!" finished Snowdrop.

"Well done for asking, Bluebell," whispered Katie, "and keep looking! There's not much time!"

Bluebell nodded and hurried back to her seat. She carried on rummaging in the pots on her table, but still didn't have any luck. She had to keep threading other beads on to her necklace, too, so that Mrs Borthwick didn't start wondering what she was up to.

Katie wished she could help, but with so many children around, they couldn't risk being seen. She glanced up at the wall clock – there were only ten minutes left of the class now. Bluebell went over to the other tables, and soon she was

searching in *their* pots too, but she still couldn't find a birthstone.

"Hurry, Bluebell, there's not much time!" Daisy hissed, but Bluebell didn't hear her over the general chatter.

"I bet I could find that bead!" said Rosehip. "It's so unfair, she gets to do everything and she can't even do it right!"

Mrs Borthwick was strolling round the class looking at everyone's work, and after a while she paused behind Bluebell. "May I?" she asked, then when Bluebell nodded she held up her necklace. "Just stop for a moment and look at this, everyone," she said. "See how Bluebell has matched the colours so beautifully and come up with the idea of knotting the thread round so that she ends up with clusters of three beads." There was a

murmur of approval from the class. "It really is wonderful," Mrs Borthwick added, handing back the necklace with care. "You're very talented at arts and crafts, dear."

Bluebell was absolutely glowing with happiness at the praise, but it was the last straw for Rosehip. With fury in her eyes she launched herself across the room and knocked over all the pots in front of Bluebell, sending beads flying everywhere! Everyone gasped – she'd been so quick it seemed as if *Bluebell* had done it.

Katie gasped – poor Bluebell. She'd be in trouble again, and just when Mrs Borthwick was saying such nice

things about her work, too!

"Bluebell, I am absolutely. . ." began Mrs Borthwick, in her had-it-up-to-here voice.

But Bluebell wasn't listening. *She* had seen the culprit. She leapt up and marched over to the sink, fists clenched, as the astonished class looked on. "How could you do that when I was finally doing well?" she shouted, seemingly at thin air. "You're just *jealous*!"

Rosehip waggled her tongue at Bluebell and hid down between the paint palettes. For a moment Bluebell seemed to forget that she was big and couldn't follow – she threw herself at the pile of palettes, sending them skittering to the floor, flinging leftover paint everywhere.

Clinging to a palette, Rosehip went tumbling through the air, then she let it

go and dived into a pile of paintings standing on a stool.

"Come out, Rosehip!" Bluebell bellowed, stamping her foot.

As all eyes were on Bluebell and her strange behaviour, Katie was the only one who noticed Snowdrop take to the air and zoom across the room. But by the time she'd started to ask her where she was going, she was already gone.

But Katie soon forgot to wonder about Snowdrop. She was too busy gaping at Bluebell, who had snatched up the paintings and was hurling each one to the floor as she searched for Rosehip. They caught

in the breeze from the open window and flipped and skittered around the room.

But Bluebell hardly noticed. "Where are you?" she shouted, whirling round to search the air. "You'll be sorry you messed with me, Rosehip!"

Snowdrop touched down beside Katie again and that was when Mrs Borthwick absolutely bellowed, "Bluebell, stop that NOW!"

It was so loud that Bluebell jumped and instantly froze.

"Bluebell, I am so disappointed in you!" the red-faced teacher continued. "Clear up those paintings IMMEDIATELY and then put all those beads back into the pots. How DARE you behave like this in my classroom, young lady!"

Bluebell hung her head and

quietly got on with picking up the paintings. Katie saw a tear plop on to the topmost one.

Once everyone was getting on with their work again, Rosehip fluttered up from her hiding place and touched down on the sink again. The others glared at her.

"I didn't mean to get Bluebell into so much trouble," she said sadly. "I just got really jealous and I couldn't help myself. I'm sorry."

"Now there's even less time to find the topaz," said Daisy reproachfully. But Rosehip looked so sorry that they couldn't stay

cross with her for long.

"Sorry, Bluebell," Rosehip whispered, but she didn't seem to hear.

When she'd cleared up the paintings, Bluebell went and put the beads away, still trying to look carefully at each one. But soon Mrs Borthwick told them all to pack away as it was home time, and Bluebell had no choice but to just shovel handfuls back into the pots. Her eyes scanned the piles of beads desperately, but she couldn't see a topaz one anywhere.

All the fairies looked as utterly miserable as Katie felt. This was the perfect chance to get another birthstone and they'd missed it.

Finally Mrs Borthwick clapped her hands and everyone clapped back. "Well, seeing as Bluebell's only with us today," she said, "she

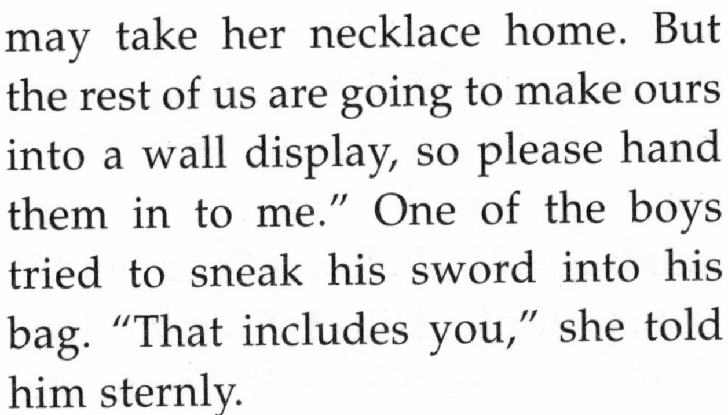

may take her necklace home. But the rest of us are going to make ours into a wall display, so please hand them in to me." One of the boys tried to sneak his sword into his bag. "That includes you," she told him sternly.

Katie watched Bluebell tying her beautiful necklace around her neck, but there was no happiness on her face. She felt so sorry for her – poor Bluebell had been so brave when she'd volunteered to turn big. It should have been fun, but instead everything had gone wrong. She hadn't got any information from Tiffany, or found a topaz bead, and she'd been in trouble all day!

Chapter 6

As everyone headed out into the playground to meet their parents, the five friends took a detour into the changing rooms. Bluebell slumped miserably on to a bench and the others fluttered down to sit beside her.

"Oh, I'm so sorry, I've completely failed!" wailed Bluebell.

They were all comforting her when suddenly the changing room door swung open. Katie and the

fairies all dived for cover behind Bluebell as someone came in.

It was absolutely the last person they were expecting to see.

It was Tiffany!

For a moment, Bluebell looked frightened, wondering what mean thing she would say or do next. But then she managed to put on a bored expression. "What do you want?" she asked sulkily.

"I've come to say sorry about being mean to you before," said Tiffany.

Bluebell blinked at her in disbelief.

"I like you now," she continued, sitting down next to Bluebell on the bench. "I've realized that you're a naughty girl like me. It was so funny when you were cheeky to Mrs Borthwick in the healthy food

lesson, and when you lied about your hair, and when you sang really loud in assembly on purpose to be rude. But best of all was when you wrecked the art room. That was brilliant!"

"I didn't mean. . ." Bluebell began, but Katie nudged her hard in the back. "Erm, yes, getting into trouble is fun," she said instead, seeing her chance to make friends with Tiffany.

"It is, isn't it?" said Tiffany gleefully. "But . . . you don't

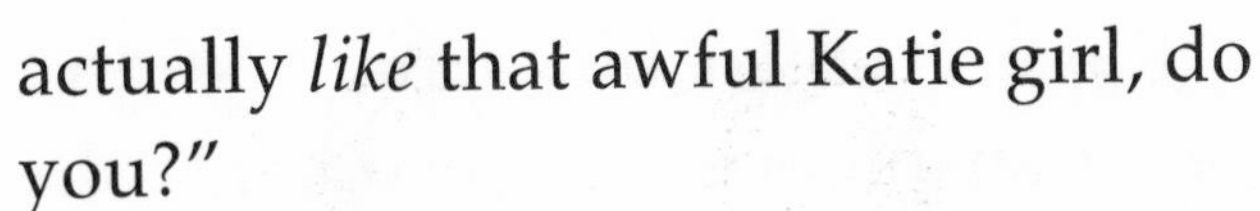

actually *like* that awful Katie girl, do you?"

Katie could see Bluebell's fists screwing up in anger at this, but then she seemed to remember her mission and smiled. "Erm, well, my school and her old school arranged this. It's just because she swapped schools that I'm here, at this lovely, erm, I mean, this yukky dump," Bluebell gabbled. "I don't even know her."

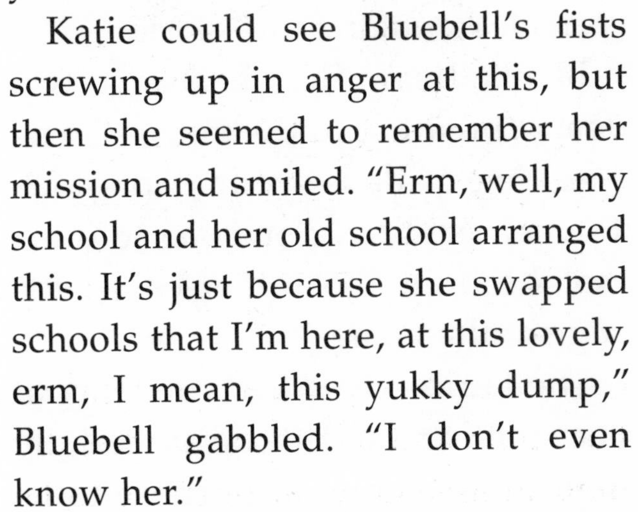

"You wouldn't want to, she's so dull!" exclaimed Tiffany, then added, "Is it really true what you said about flying to school?"

"Erm, yes, because, erm. . ." Bluebell paused to think of a human-sounding answer, as Katie has taught her. "Because my dad's very rich, he's got a helichopper," she finished.

Katie cringed but Tiffany didn't seem suspicious. "Helicopter," she corrected, looking impressed.

Bluebell saw her chance, took a deep breath, and said, "Erm, speaking of dads, your dad's Max Towner, isn't he? Someone told me that he built those houses on the edge of the village."

The fairies all smiled excitedly at one another as Tiffany puffed up with pride.

"Yes, he did," she replied. "He's building loads more too. There's a scrap of rough ground with a stupid old oak tree on, and he's going to build a luxury villa on it. If I throw a big enough tantrum I bet he'll let me sit in the bulldozer and pull the lever too! I can't wait to see that old hunk of wood come crashing down!"

Bluebell gasped in horror, then

quickly turned it into a pretend yelp of excitement. "And when will this happen?" she managed to ask.

"I don't know," said Tiffany. "Daddy says the exact date has to be Top Secret in case some stupid tree huggers find out about it and start a protest."

"Oh, right," said Bluebell.

"Anyway, I have to go," said Tiffany. "I'm going shopping – Mum's buying me a new dress, well, probably two."

"Erm, yes, right – I have to go and buy some more different dresses too," said Bluebell uncertainly. "But first I have to change. See you later."

Of course, Tiffany didn't realize that she meant change back into a fairy! With a big smile at Bluebell and an invite to come back any time, she left.

When the door had swung shut again, Katie and the fairies came out and leapt on to Bluebell's lap.

"Well done, Bluebell!" Snowdrop squealed. "Now we know for sure that Max Towner is the culprit!"

"We just have to find out when he's planning to knock down the tree!" cried Rosehip.

"We're so proud of you, Bluebell," added Daisy.

Bluebell couldn't help smiling. She was quite proud of herself too! "We didn't find the topaz, though," she said with a sigh.

"Yes, we did," said Snowdrop. She spoke so softly that no one paid any attention at first. "We got it," she repeated, louder, and they all turned to gape at her.

Smiling, she reached into the pocket of her purple petal skirt and

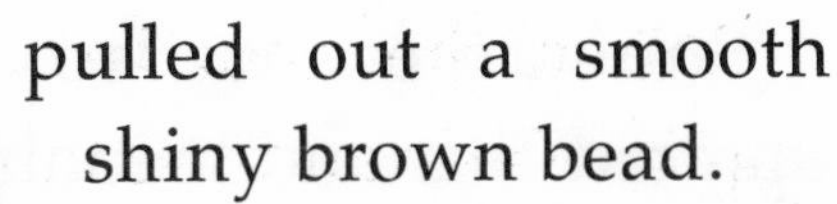

pulled out a smooth shiny brown bead.

Daisy, Rosehip and Katie leapt on her, hugging her tight!

"Oh, Snowdrop! Well done!" cried Bluebell.

"But how?" asked Daisy when they broke apart.

"When?" said Rosehip, gaping.

"When Bluebell was making a scene by the sink trying to get hold of you, everyone was so distracted that I knew I could fly over and search among the spilt beads," Snowdrop explained.

Katie grinned. "So that's what you were up to!"

Snowdrop smiled shyly. "I spotted this and it looked the right colour for topaz, so I grabbed it," she said. "I suppose it was lucky that Rosehip and Bluebell were fighting after all!"

"But we weren't really!" Rosehip told Snowdrop. "I guessed that you were planning to search for a bead, that's why I created a diversion!"

"And I pretended to get really cross with Rosehip so that everyone would look at me, to give you time to get across the room and grab the bead!" Bluebell insisted.

They gave each other a hug as if to prove it.

Katie stifled a giggle and Daisy raised her eyebrows. "Of course you did," she said. "Whatever you say."

"Now, quickly, we have to change back, Mum will be waiting," said

Katie. She felt sad about losing her beautiful shimmering fairy wings, of course, but the thought of Mum waiting in the playground for her more than made up for it.

Bluebell lay along the bench and once Snowdrop had sprinkled Katie's and Bluebell's palms with fairy dust, they pressed them tightly together.

This time, Katie was expecting the lightning zap, but it still jolted her. Then a loud POP! brought her back to her normal size. She shook her arms and legs, while a fairy-sized Bluebell fluttered her wings and did a few happy fairy hops. "It's nice to be me again!" they both said at once, making everyone laugh.

"Oh no!" cried Katie, pointing at Bluebell's neck. "You should have taken off my tie – how on earth am I going to explain that to Mum!"

They all laughed again as Bluebell handed Katie the teeny-weeny tie, which she wove round her wrist like a bracelet.

Then Katie hurried out into the playground, with the fairies stowed safely in her school bag. After the biggest hug, she pulled Mum quickly away before anyone from her class could spot her and wonder what she was doing there! On the way home, Mum asked Katie what she'd done that day. Katie smiled a mysterious smile and said, "Well, we were dancing in music and movement and it felt like I was flying."

Mum squeezed her hand. "I've always wanted to fly," she said dreamily. "Can you imagine it, darling? Soaring and twirling and dancing in the air? Wouldn't it be wonderful?"

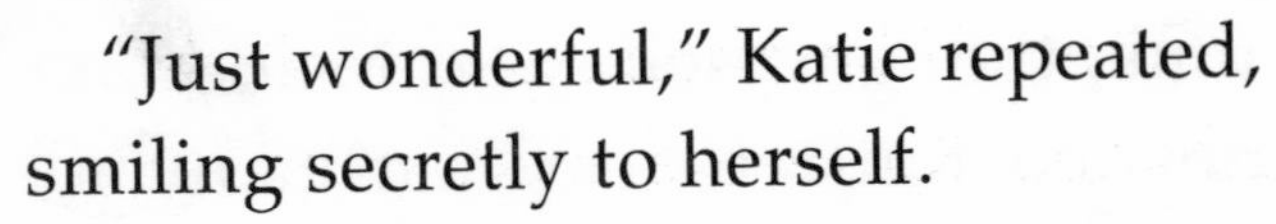

"Just wonderful," Katie repeated, smiling secretly to herself.

As soon as she got home, Katie galloped upstairs to stow the topaz bead safely away in her jewellery box with the garnet ring. Only ten more birthstones to find and they'd be able to save the tree!

Then, after a welcome snack of apple juice and carrot cake with Mum (missing lunch had left her very hungry!) she hurried out to the Fairy House.

Once Katie had shrunk down to fairy size (no wings this

time, though!) she went inside. But no one ran to greet her. "Anyone home?" she called. Still nothing. Then she heard some muffled giggling and a voice called down the stairs, "Hide and seek! You're it!"

Katie grinned and stomped up the stairs, calling, "I'm coming to get you!" It didn't take her long to find the fairies, as they were no good at keeping still *or* being quiet!

Soon she'd pulled Bluebell out of the empty bath, prised Snowdrop from her wardrobe, discovered Rosehip under her bed and found Daisy squashed into a kitchen cupboard!

After a few more games, they all lay in a line on Bluebell's polka-dot bedspread, their heads dangling over the edge.

"I wish *I* could have been big!" said Daisy,

with a sigh. "I didn't say so before because I didn't want to cause any falling out, but it all looked such fun – especially the music and movement!"

"I think we all wish we could have done that!" said Snowdrop ruefully.

"I know, we can have our own class, right here!" cried Rosehip.

"What a brilliant idea!" Bluebell giggled. "And this time I won't get told off and have to sit out!"

"You might!" said Rosehip cheekily.

"I won't!" countered Bluebell. "Because *this time* I'm going to be the teacher, and I won't tell *myself* off, so there!"

Laughing, they pulled each other into the living room and pushed the rose-petal sofas and dandelion rugs

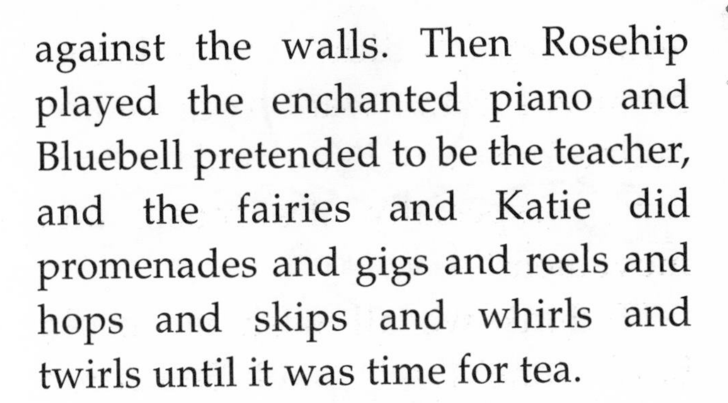

against the walls. Then Rosehip played the enchanted piano and Bluebell pretended to be the teacher, and the fairies and Katie did promenades and gigs and reels and hops and skips and whirls and twirls until it was time for tea.

The End

Bluebell

Spring fairy

Likes:

blue, blue, blue and more blue,
turning somersaults in the air, dancing

Dislikes:

coming second, being told what to do

Daisy

Summer fairy

Likes:

everyone to be friends, bright sunshine,
cheery yellow colours, smiling

Dislikes:

arguments, cold dark places,
orange nylon dresses

Rosehip

Autumn fairy

Likes:

riding magic ponies, telling Bluebell what to do, playing the piano, singing

Dislikes:

keeping quiet, boring colours, not being the centre of attention!

Snowdrop

Winter fairy

Likes:

singing fairy songs, cool quiet places, riding her favourite magical unicorn, making snowfairies

Dislikes:

being too hot, keeping secrets

Don't miss book three!